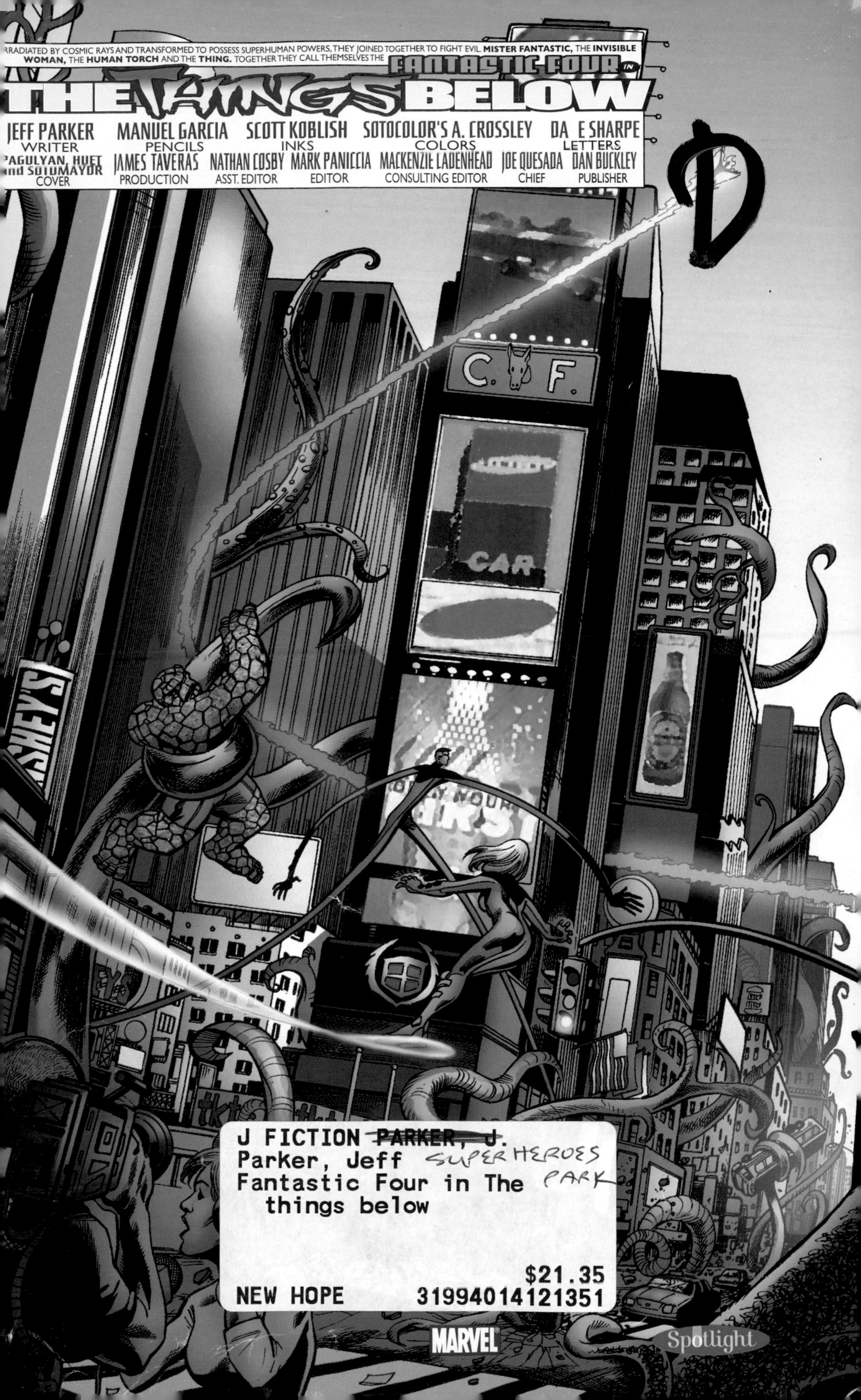
RRADIATED BY COSMIC RAYS AND TRANSFORMED TO POSSESS SUPERHUMAN POWERS, THEY JOINED TOGETHER TO FIGHT EVIL. MISTER FANTASTIC, THE INVISIBLE WOMAN, THE HUMAN TORCH AND THE THING. TOGETHER THEY CALL THEMSELVES THE FANTASTIC FOUR IN
THE THINGS BELOW
JEFF PARKER WRITER
MANUEL GARCIA PENCILS
SCOTT KOBLISH INKS
SOTOCOLOR'S A. CROSSLEY COLORS
DA E SHARPE LETTERS
PAGULYAN, HUET and SOTOMAYOR COVER
JAMES TAVERAS PRODUCTION
NATHAN COSBY ASST. EDITOR
MARK PANICCIA EDITOR
MACKENZIE CADENHEAD CONSULTING EDITOR
JOE QUESADA CHIEF
DAN BUCKLEY PUBLISHER
C. F.
CAR
MARVEL
Spotlight

VISIT US AT
www.abdopublishing.com

Spotlight library bound edition © 2007. Spotlight is a division of ABDO Publishing Company, Edina, Minnesota.

Cataloging Data

Parker, Jeff
    Fantastic Four in the things below / Jeff Parker, writer ; Manuel Garcia, pencils ; Scott Koblish, inks. -- Library bound ed.
      p. cm. -- (Fantastic Four)
    Summary: Irradiated by cosmic rays and transformed to possess superhuman powers, Mr. Fantastic, the Invisible Woman, the Human Torch, and the Thing join together to fight evil.
    "Marvel age"--Cover.
    Revision of the January 2006 issue of Marvel adventures Fantastic Four.
    ISBN-13: 978-1-59961-205-8
    ISBN-10: 1-59961-205-4
    1. Fantastic Four (Fictitious characters)--Comic books, strips, etc.--Fiction. 2. Graphic novels. I. Title. II. Title: The things below   III. Series.

    741.5dc22

All Spotlight books are reinforced library binding
and manufactured in the United States of America

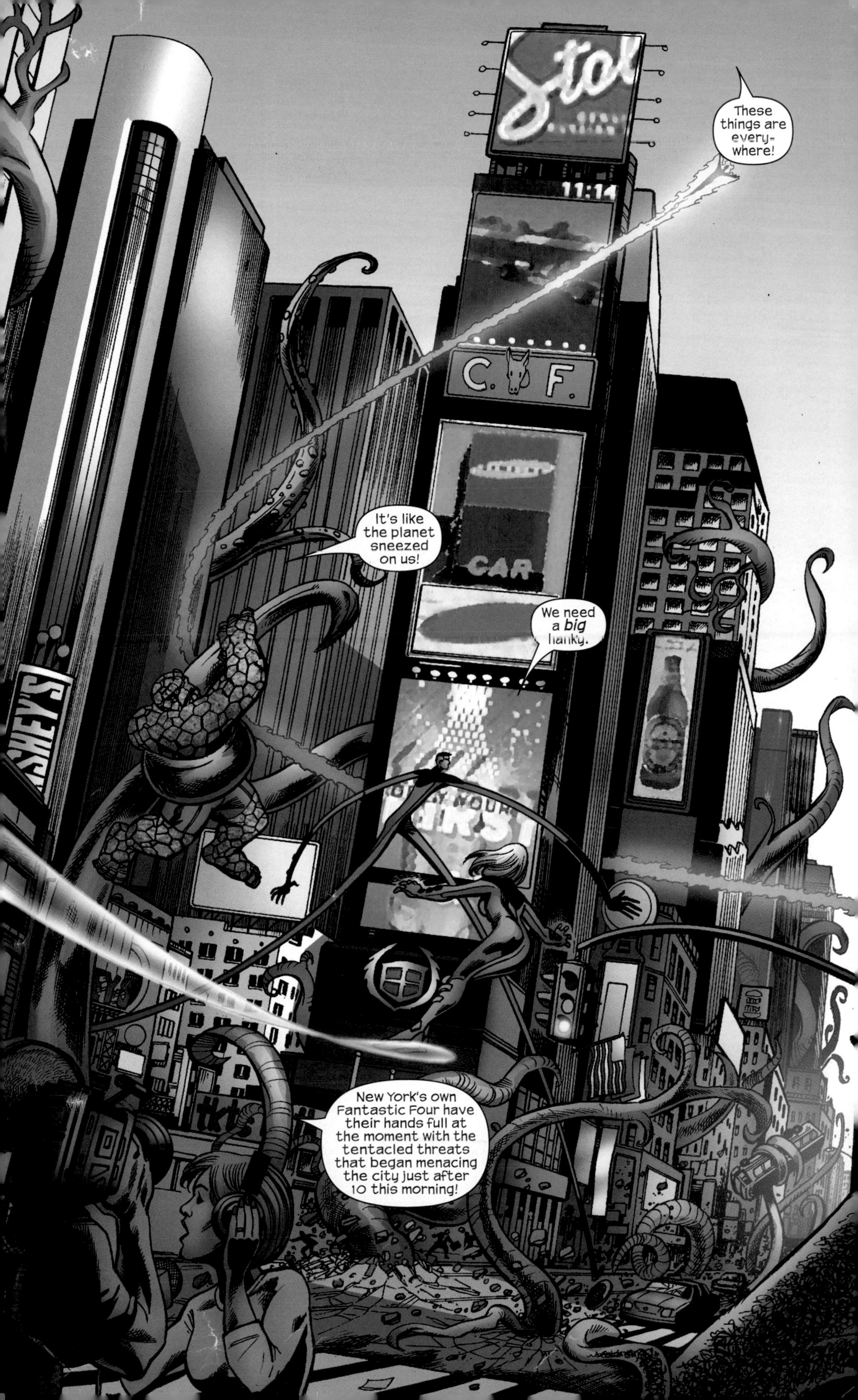
These things are every-where!
It's like the planet sneezed on us!
We need a *big* hanky.
New York's own Fantastic Four have their hands full at the moment with the tentacled threats that began menacing the city just after 10 this morning!

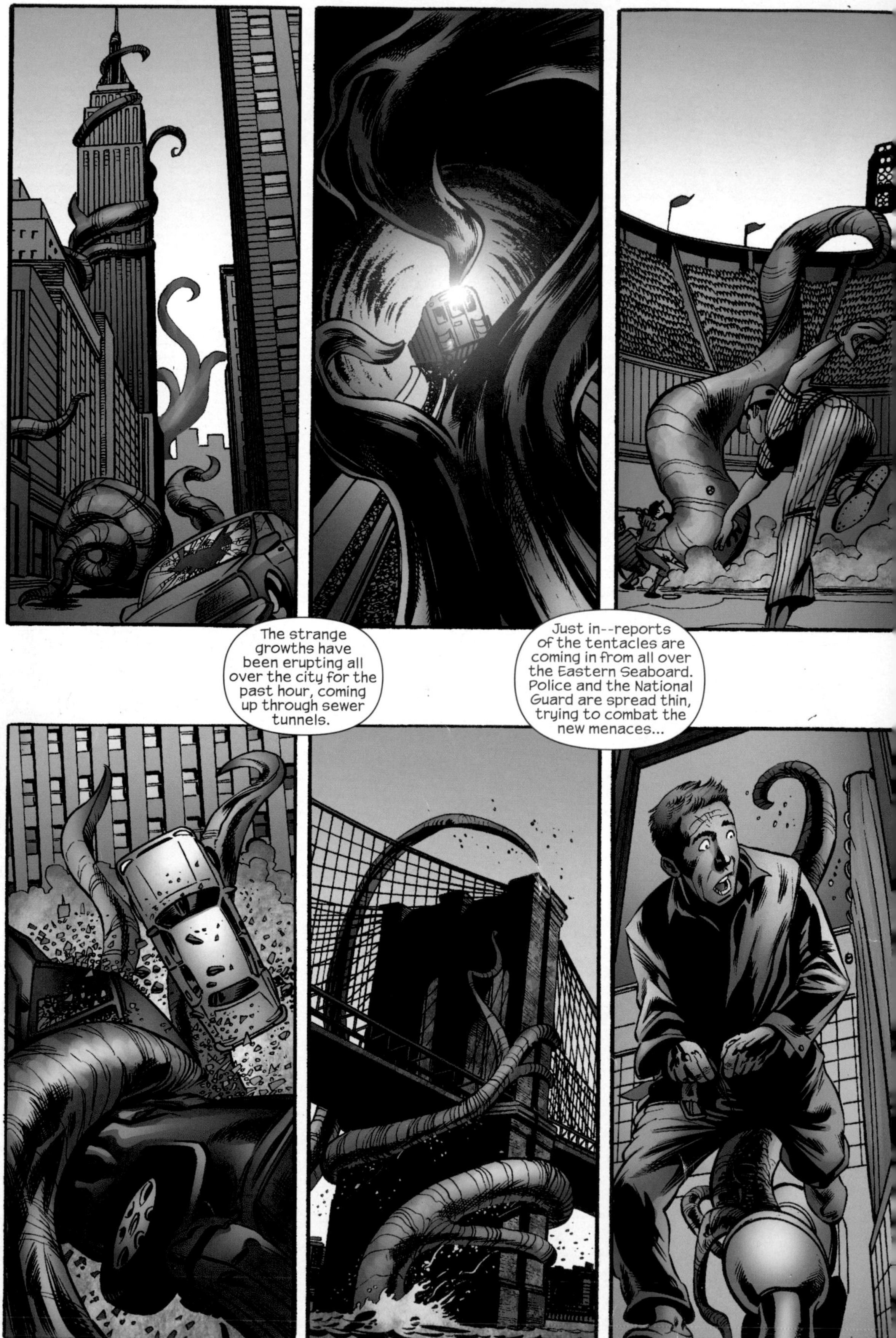
The strange growths have been erupting all over the city for the past hour, coming up through sewer tunnels.
Just in--reports of the tentacles are coming in from all over the Eastern Seaboard. Police and the National Guard are spread thin, trying to combat the new menaces...

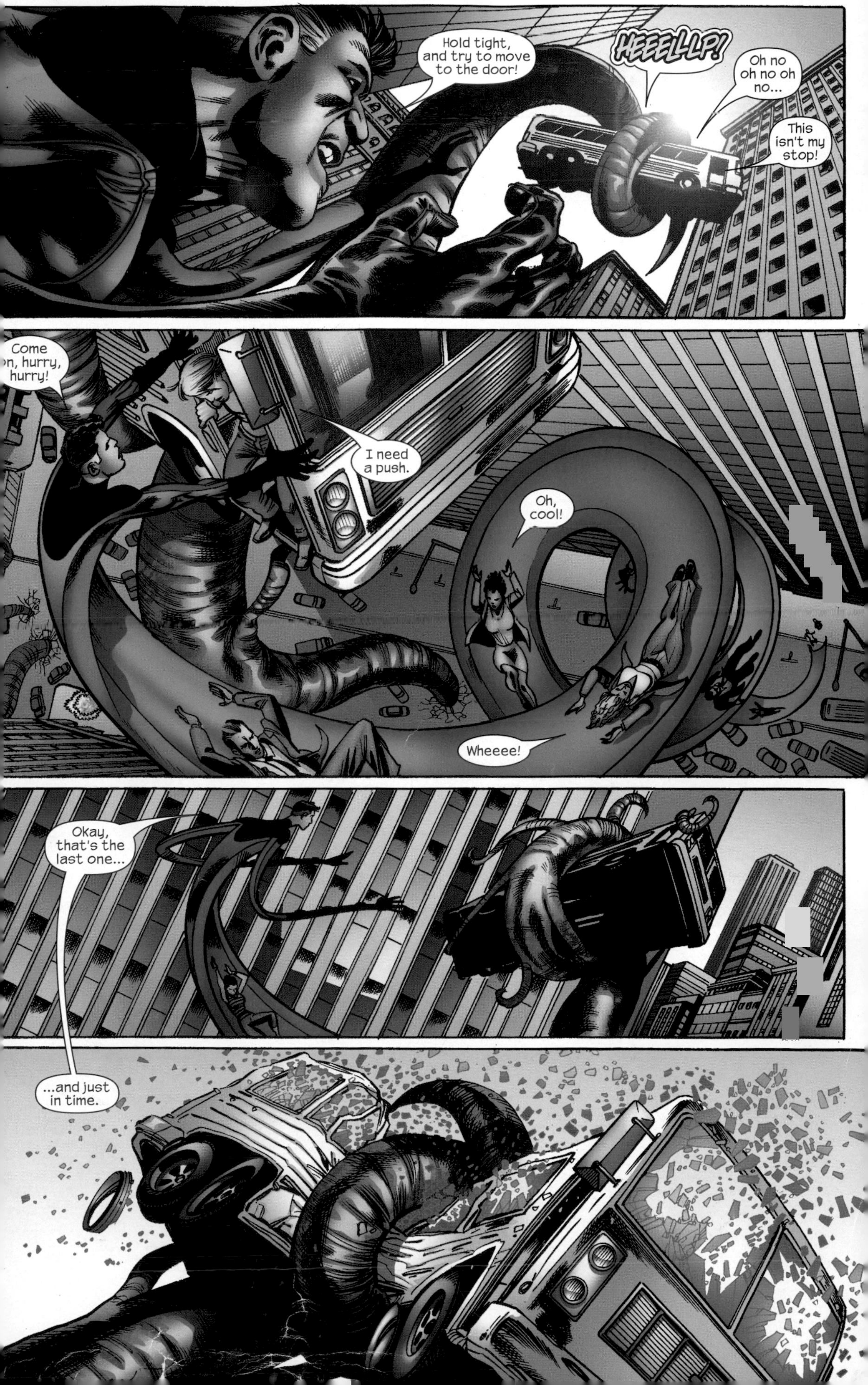
Hold tight, and try to move to the door!
HEEELLLP!
Oh no oh no oh no...
This isn't my stop!
Come on, hurry, hurry!
I need a push.
Oh, cool!
Wheeee!
Okay, that's the last one...
...and just in time.

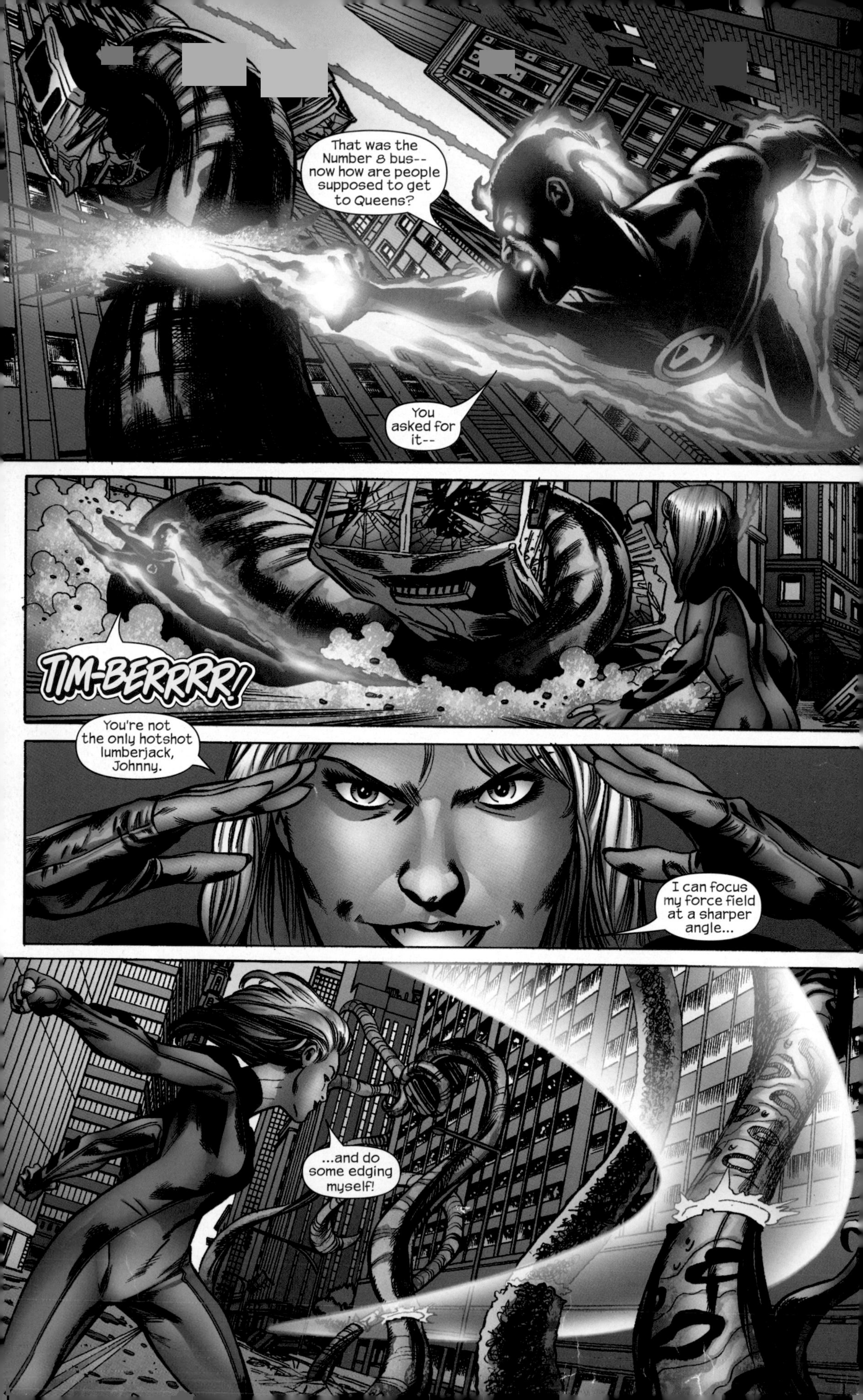
That was the Number 8 bus--now how are people supposed to get to Queens?
You asked for it--
TIM-BERRRR!
You're not the only hotshot lumberjack, Johnny.
I can focus my force field at a sharper angle...
...and do some edging myself!

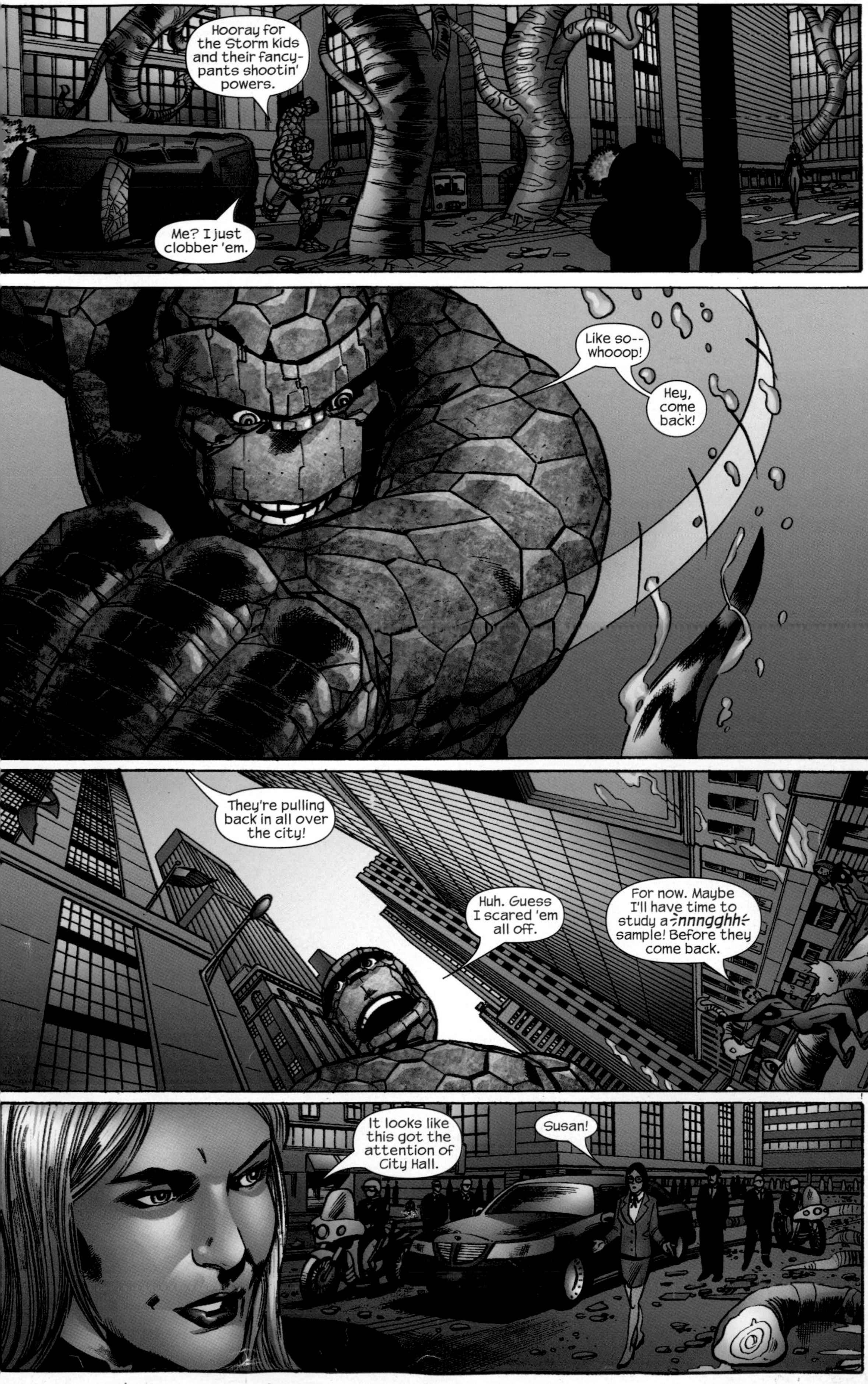
Hooray for the Storm kids and their fancy-pants shootin' powers.
Me? I just clobber 'em.
Like so--whooop!
Hey, come back!
They're pulling back in all over the city!
Huh. Guess I scared 'em all off.
For now. Maybe I'll have time to study a nnngghh sample! Before they come back.
It looks like this got the attention of City Hall.
Susan!

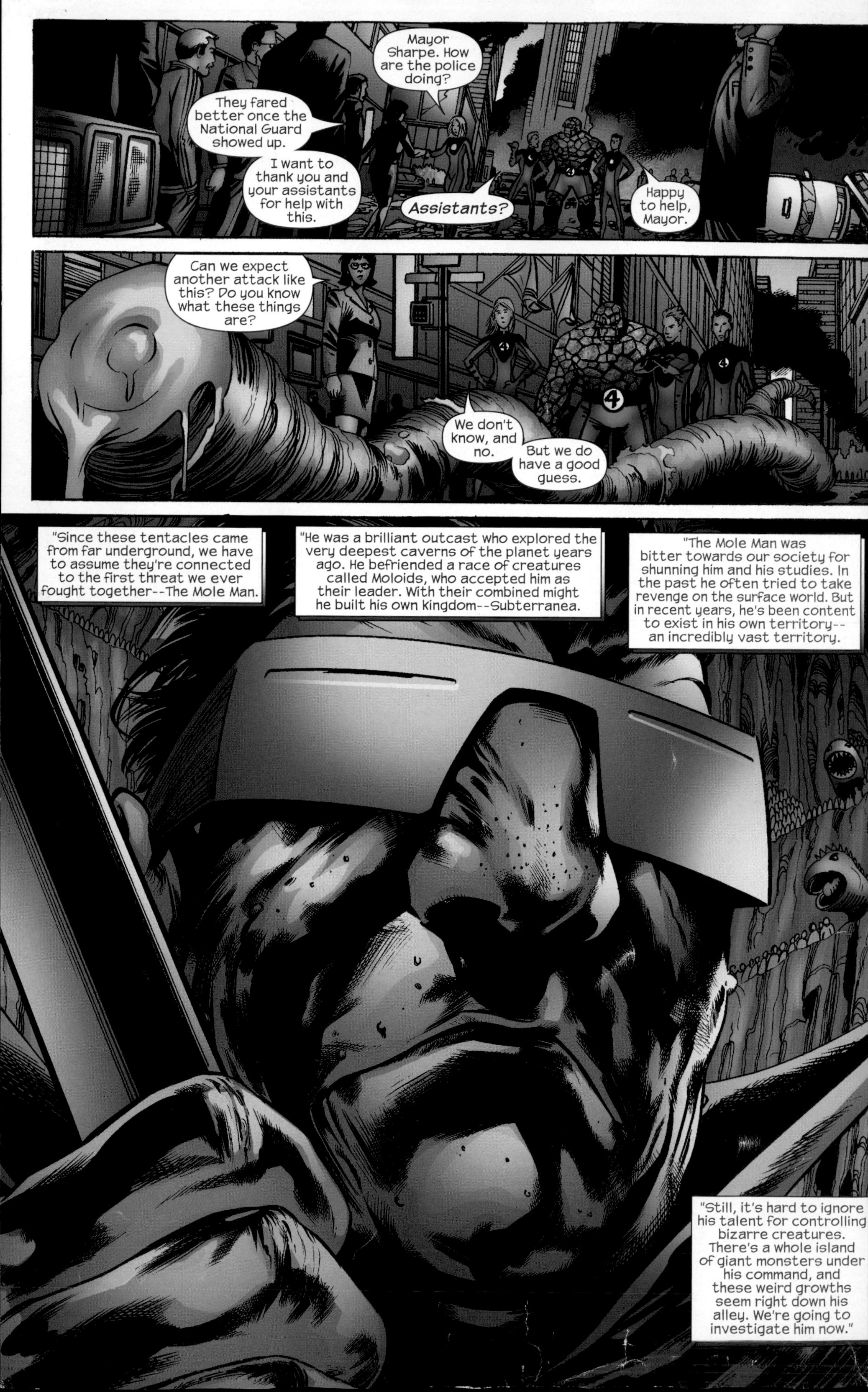
Mayor Sharpe. How are the police doing?
They fared better once the National Guard showed up.
I want to thank you and your assistants for help with this.
Assistants?
Happy to help, Mayor.
Can we expect another attack like this? Do you know what these things are?
We don't know, and no.
But we do have a good guess.
"Since these tentacles came from far underground, we have to assume they're connected to the first threat we ever fought together--The Mole Man.
"He was a brilliant outcast who explored the very deepest caverns of the planet years ago. He befriended a race of creatures called Moloids, who accepted him as their leader. With their combined might he built his own kingdom--Subterranea.
"The Mole Man was bitter towards our society for shunning him and his studies. In the past he often tried to take revenge on the surface world. But in recent years, he's been content to exist in his own territory--an incredibly vast territory.
"Still, it's hard to ignore his talent for controlling bizarre creatures. There's a whole island of giant monsters under his command, and these weird growths seem right down his alley. We're going to investigate him now."

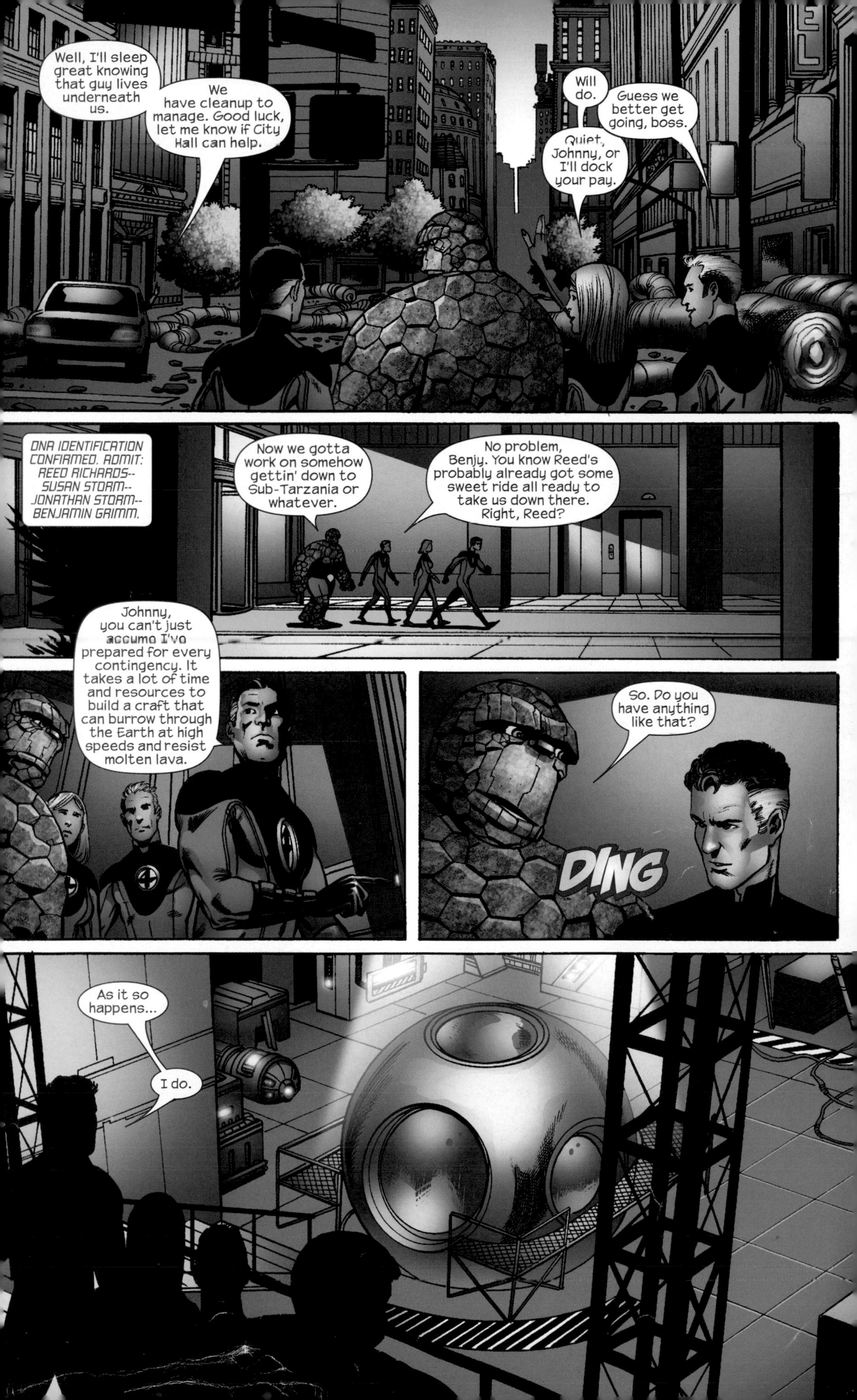
Well, I'll sleep great knowing that guy lives underneath us.
We have cleanup to manage. Good luck, let me know if City Hall can help.
Will do.
Guess we better get going, boss.
Quiet, Johnny, or I'll dock your pay.
DNA IDENTIFICATION CONFIRMED. ADMIT: REED RICHARDS-- SUSAN STORM-- JONATHAN STORM-- BENJAMIN GRIMM.
Now we gotta work on somehow gettin' down to Sub-Tarzania or whatever.
No problem, Benjy. You know Reed's probably already got some sweet ride all ready to take us down there. Right, Reed?
Johnny, you can't just assume I've prepared for every contingency. It takes a lot of time and resources to build a craft that can burrow through the Earth at high speeds and resist molten lava.
So. Do you have anything like that?
DING
As it so happens...
I do.

Everyone strapped in?

Yeah, but Ben seems to be in the driver's seat-- *again.*

That's 'cause I'm the pilot of the group, junior. We're not going through the *air.* Besides, I'm like the big-time stunt-driver!

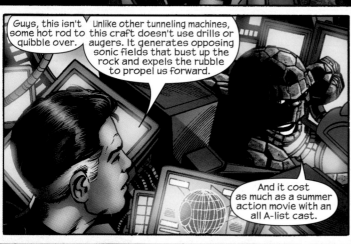

Guys, this isn't some hot rod to quibble over.

Unlike other tunneling machines, this craft doesn't use drills or augers. It generates opposing sonic fields that bust up the rock and expels the rubble to propel us forward.

And it cost as much as a summer action movie with an all A-list cast.

Now Johnny, if you want, you can engage the sonic drive.

Cool!

WWHHHRRRRRMMMN

WAAAAAHHHHHOoOo!

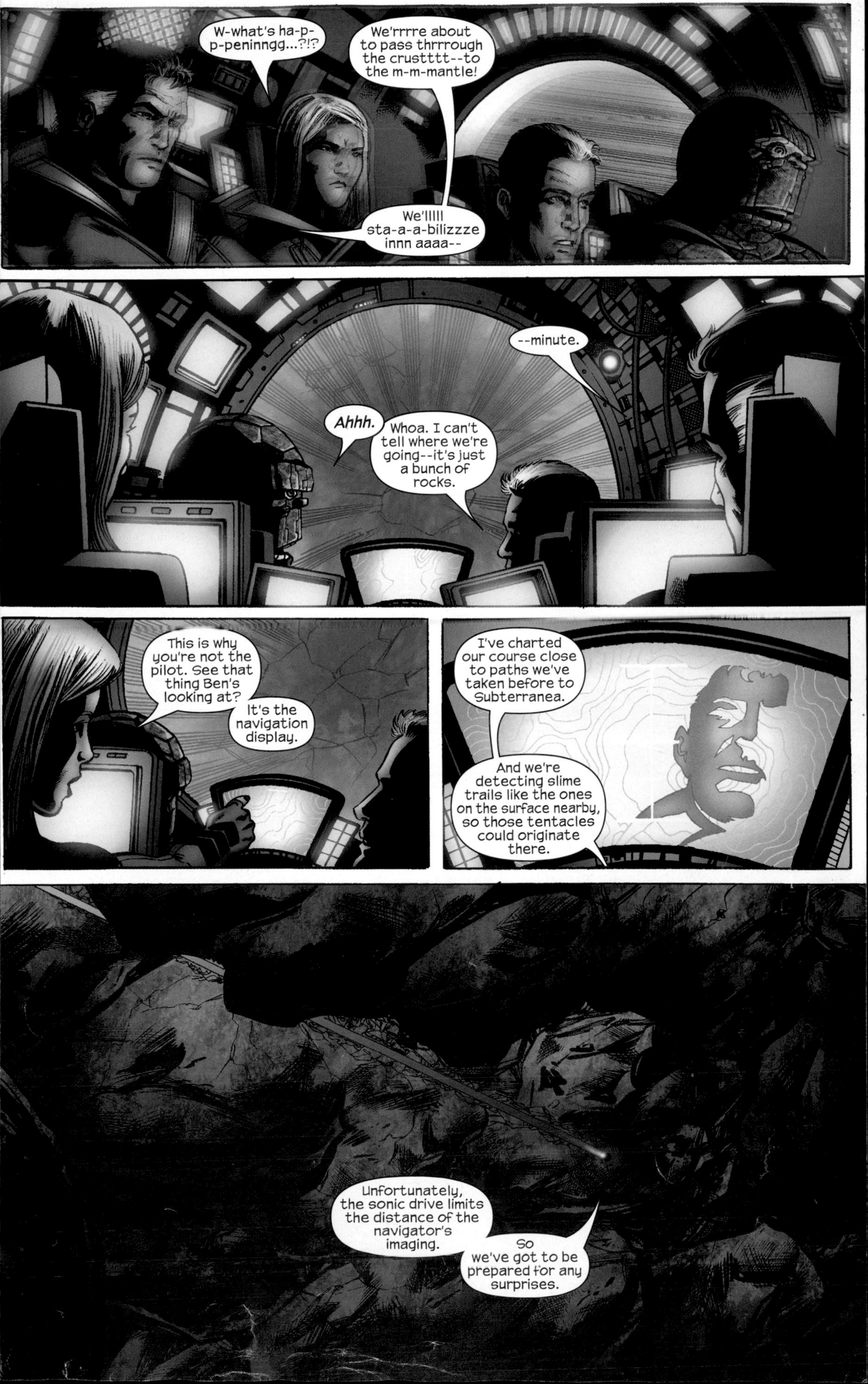
W-what's ha-p-p-peninngg...?!?
We'rrrre about to pass thrrrough the crusttttt--to the m-m-mantle!
We'lllll sta-a-a-bilizzze innn aaaa--
--minute.
Ahhh.
Whoa. I can't tell where we're going--it's just a bunch of rocks.
This is why you're not the pilot. See that thing Ben's looking at?
It's the navigation display.
I've charted our course close to paths we've taken before to Subterranea.
And we're detecting slime trails like the ones on the surface nearby, so those tentacles could originate there.
Unfortunately, the sonic drive limits the distance of the navigator's imaging.
So we've got to be prepared for any surprises.

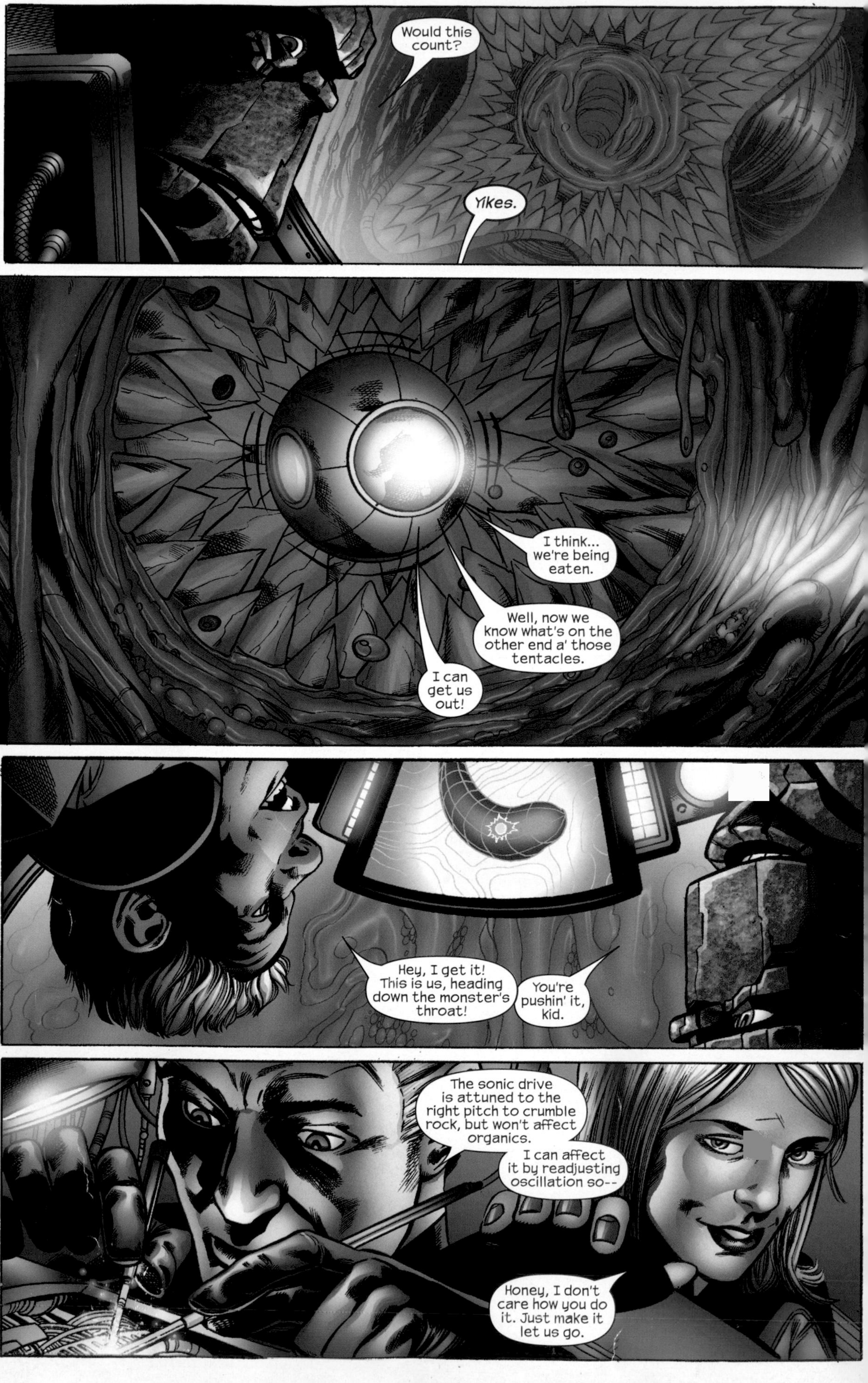
Would this count?
Yikes.
I think... we're being eaten.
Well, now we know what's on the other end a' those tentacles.
I can get us out!
Hey, I get it! This is us, heading down the monster's throat!
You're pushin' it, kid.
The sonic drive is attuned to the right pitch to crumble rock, but won't affect organics.
I can affect it by readjusting oscillation so--
Honey, I don't care how you do it. Just make it let us go.

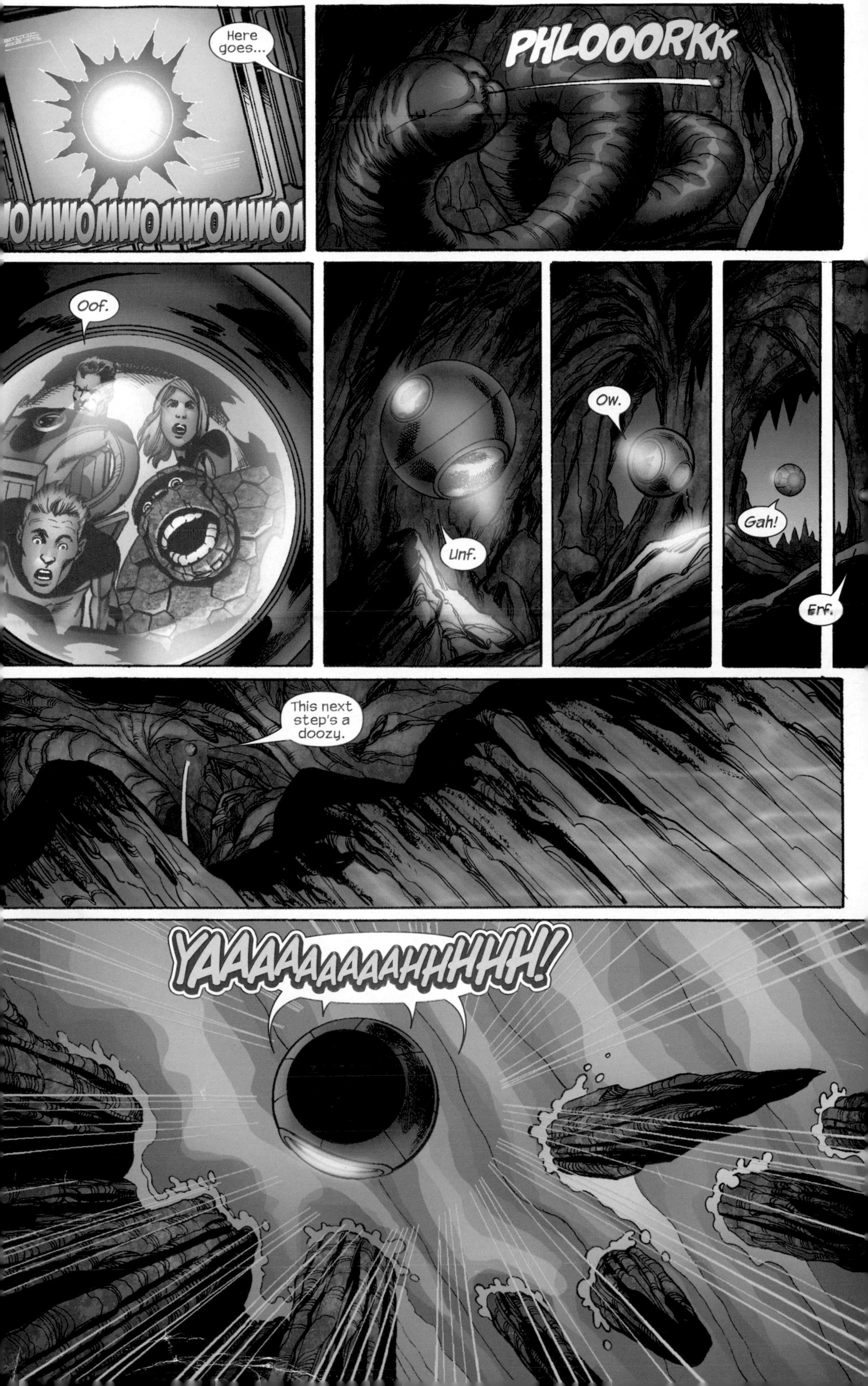
Here goes...
WOMWOMWOMWOMWOM
PHLOOORKK
Oof.
Unf.
Ow.
Gah!
Erf.
This next step's a doozy.
YAAAAAAAAAHHHHH!

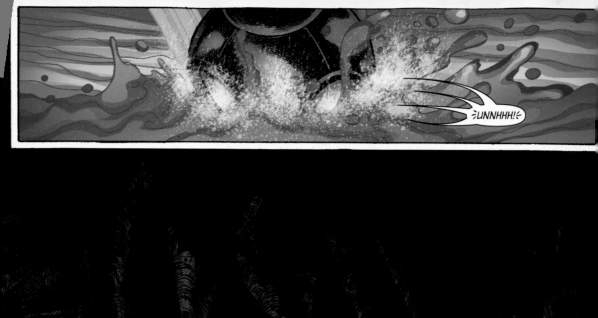

‹UNNHHH!›

Wow.
Now...is this
somewhere we
want to be?

Yeah, we're not
far from Subta--
Sub---the Mole
Man's place.

The
steam's a dead
giveaway.

Maneuver us
up into the stream,
Ben. That feeds
directly into
the city.

This lava flow
should come really
close to an under-
ground river.
There.

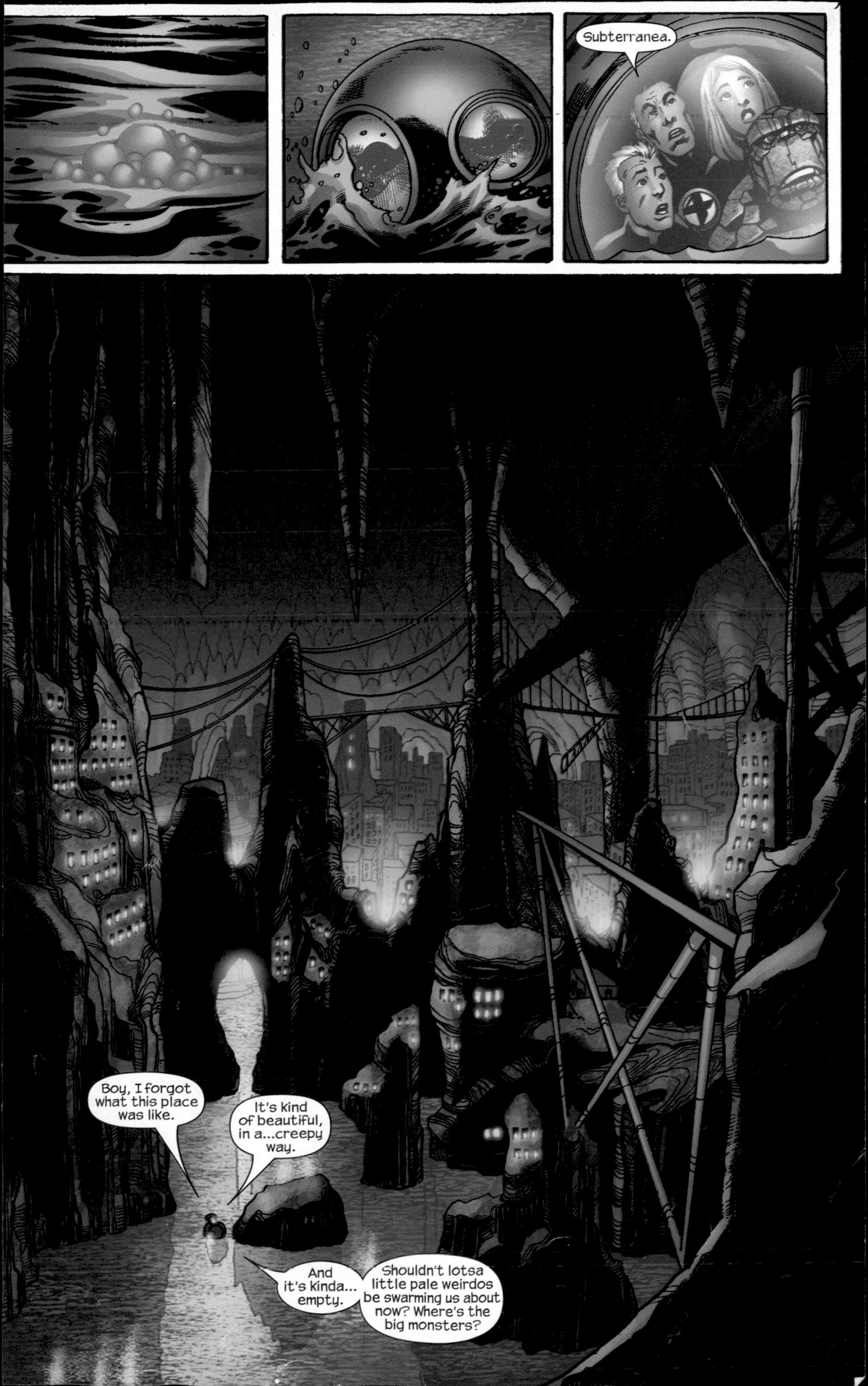
Subterranea.
Boy, I forgot what this place was like.
It's kind of beautiful, in a...creepy way.
And it's kinda... empty.
Shouldn't lotsa little pale weirdos be swarming us about now? Where's the big monsters?

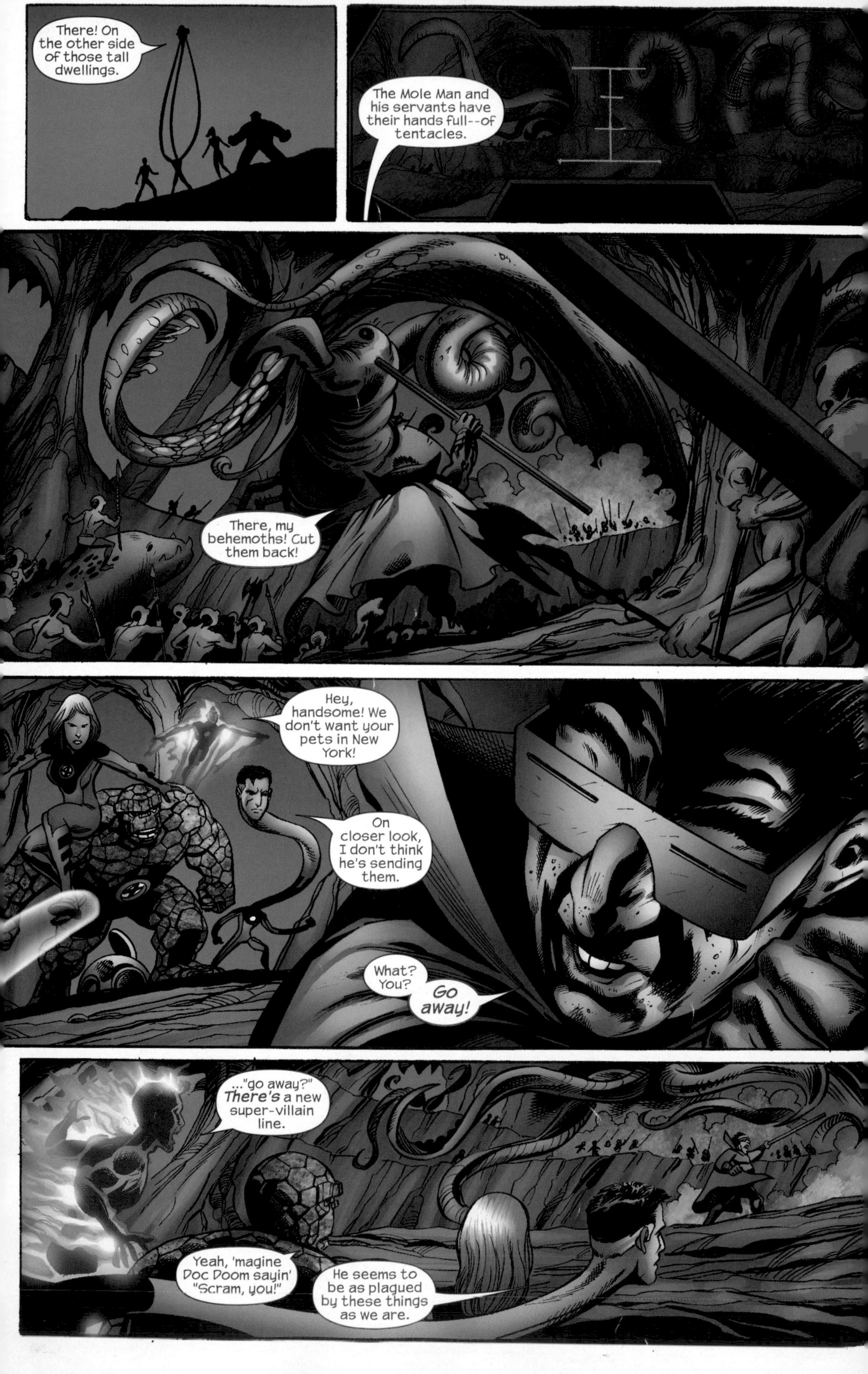
There! On the other side of those tall dwellings.
The Mole Man and his servants have their hands full--of tentacles.
There, my behemoths! Cut them back!
Hey, handsome! We don't want your pets in New York!
On closer look, I don't think he's sending them.
What? You? Go away!
..."go away?" There's a new super-villain line.
Yeah, 'magine Doc Doom sayin' "Scram, you!"
He seems to be as plagued by these things as we are.

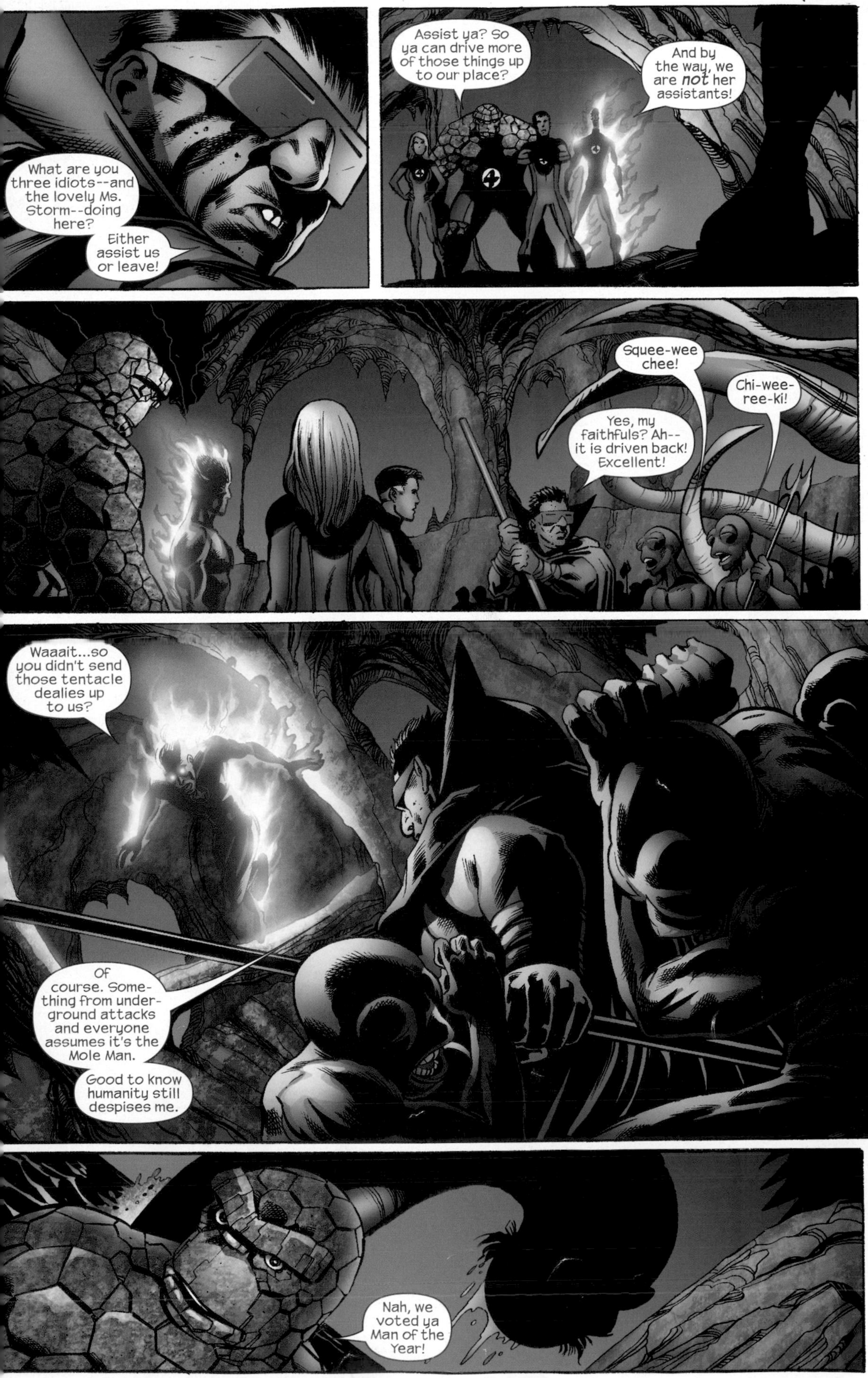
What are you three idiots--and the lovely Ms. Storm--doing here?
Either assist us or leave!
Assist ya? So ya can drive more of those things up to our place?
And by the way, we are *not* her assistants!
Squee-wee chee!
Chi-wee-ree-ki!
Yes, my faithfuls? Ah--it is driven back! Excellent!
Waaait...so you didn't send those tentacle dealies up to us?
Of course. Something from underground attacks and everyone assumes it's the Mole Man.
Good to know humanity still despises me.
Nah, we voted ya Man of the Year!

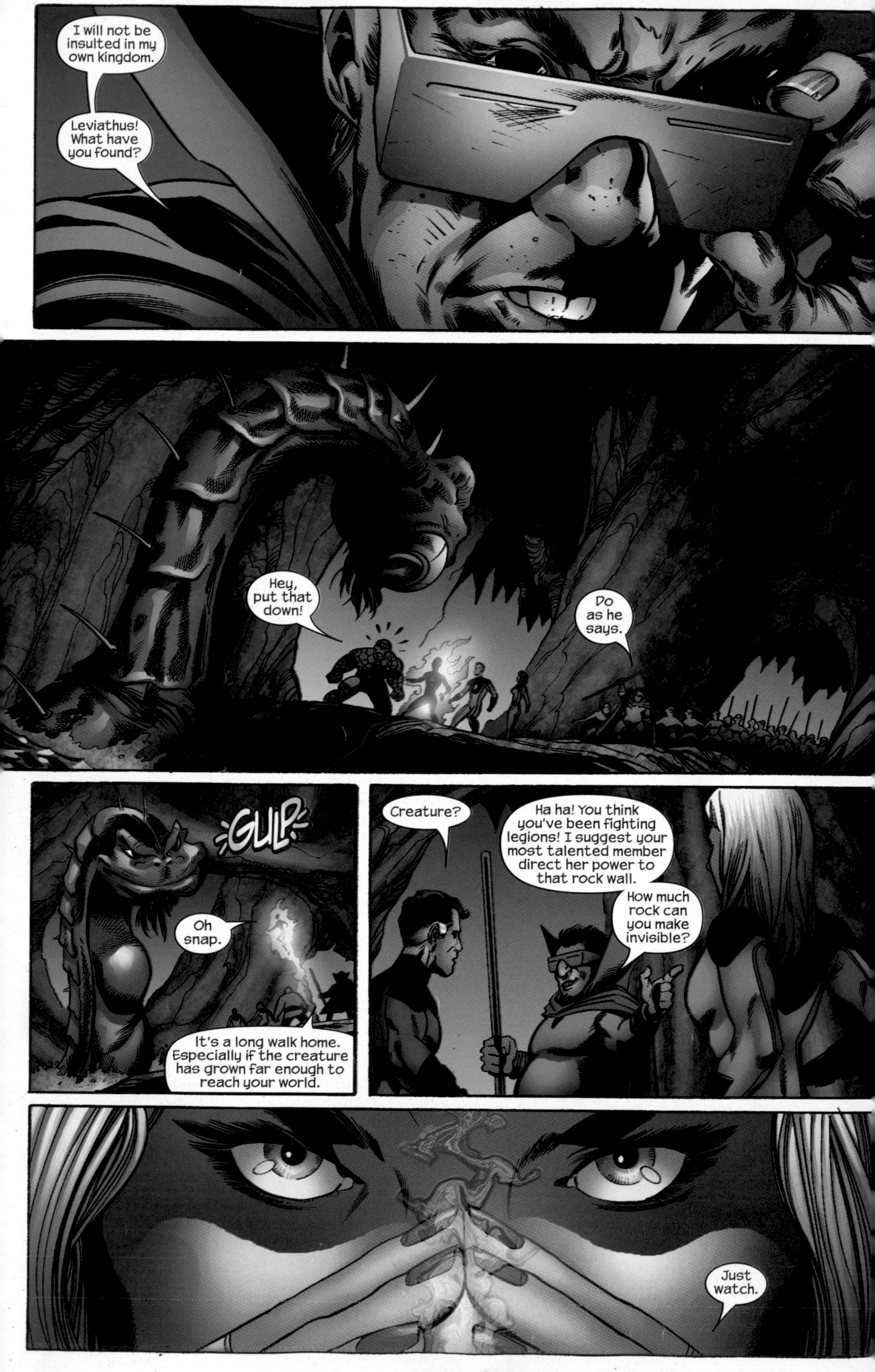
I will not be insulted in my own kingdom.
Leviathus! What have you found?
Hey, put that down!
Do as he says.
GULP
Oh snap.
It's a long walk home. Especially if the creature has grown far enough to reach your world.
Creature?
Ha ha! You think you've been fighting legions! I suggest your most talented member direct her power to that rock wall.
How much rock can you make invisible?
Just watch.

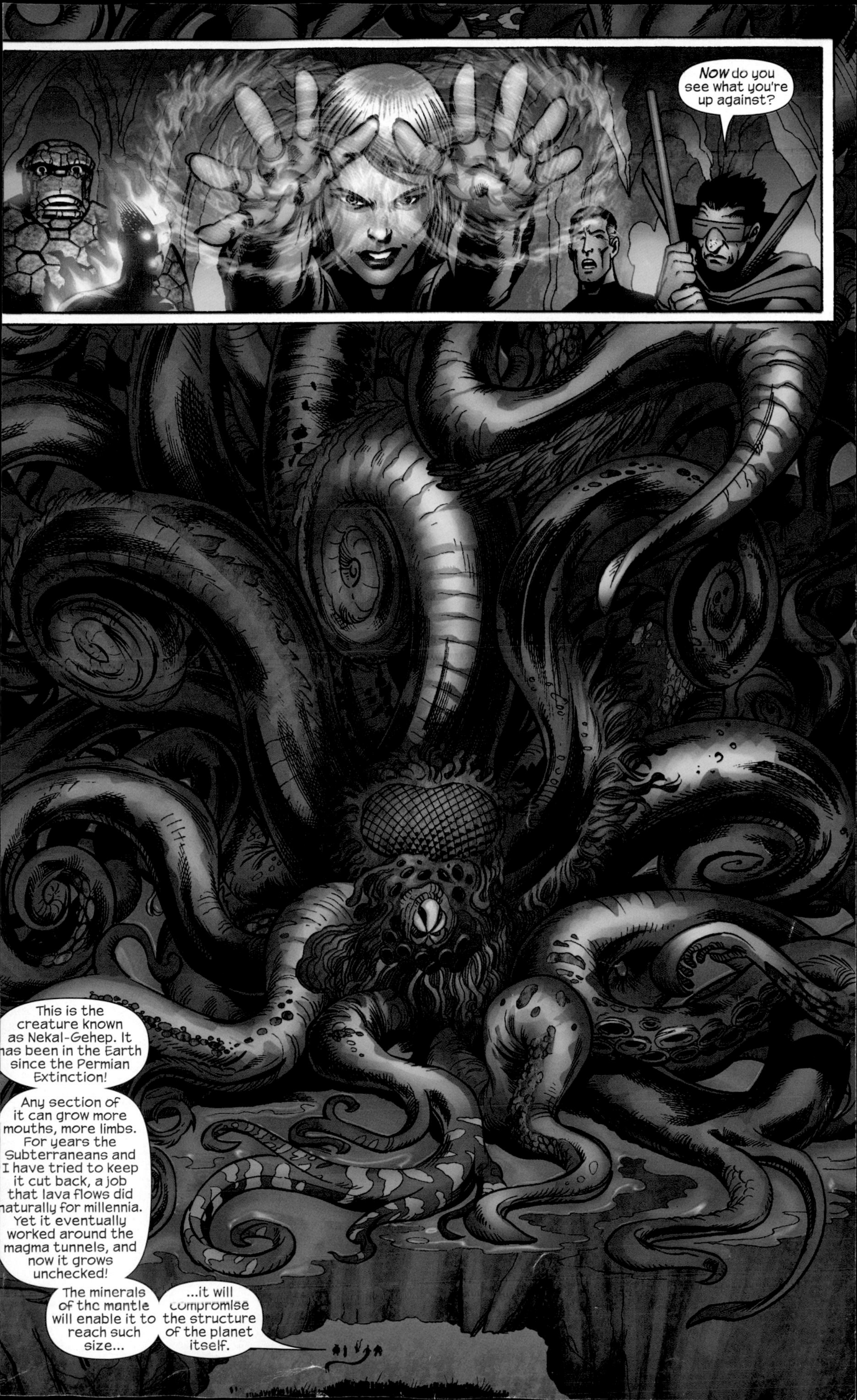

NOW do you see what you're up against?
This is the creature known as Nekal-Gehep. It as been in the Earth since the Permian Extinction!
Any section of it can grow more mouths, more limbs. For years the Subterraneans and I have tried to keep it cut back, a job that lava flows did aturally for millennia. Yet it eventually worked around the magma tunnels, and now it grows unchecked!
The minerals of the mantle will enable it to reach such size...
...it will compromise the structure of the planet itself.

How... could that happen?

It's growing geometrically. That means it's not just adding mass, it's multiplying it. We were just seeing a section of it too...it must be the size of New Zealand now!

I...can't clobber that.

I am loath to harm such a venerable old creature, but it has run its course.

Come, my troops. We must *kill* Nekal-Gehep.

NO! This animal has made Earth its home longer than all our species! We can't just kill it.

Hey Stretch, I'm with ya on settin' spiders free and all, but the Mole Man's right on this one.

Yeah, we have to protect the planet first.

Enough talk! We must destroy the creature!

But it might be possible to save it. We have to try.

Susan is right! We must save the creature!

Your Highness, how did you think you would kill it?

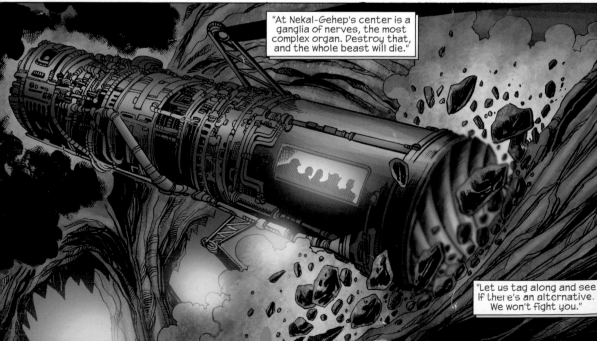

"At Nekal-Gehep's center is a ganglia of nerves, the most complex organ. Destroy that, and the whole beast will die."

"Let us tag along and see if there's an alternative. We won't fight you."

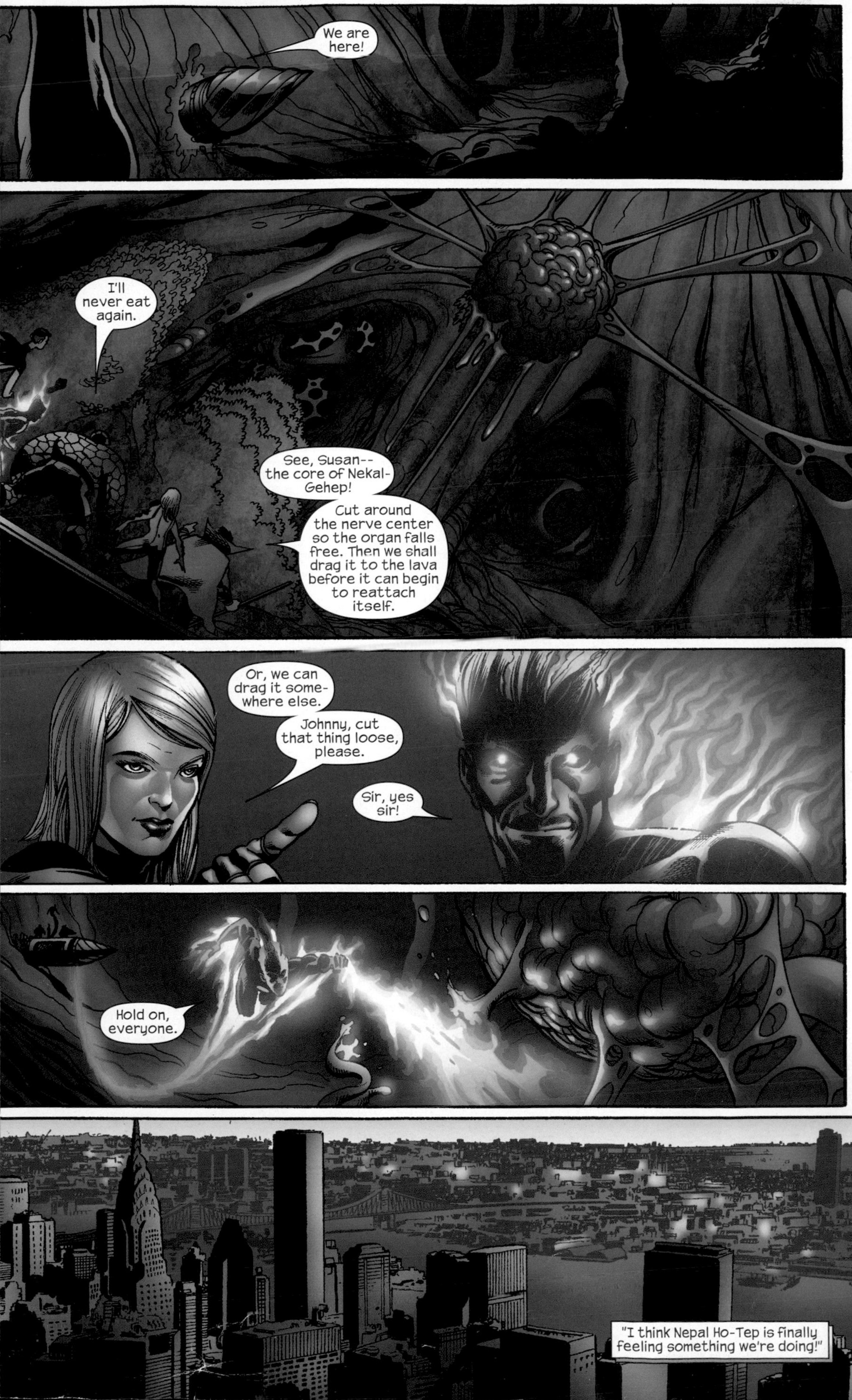
We are here!
I'll never eat again.
See, Susan-- the core of Nekal-Gehep!
Cut around the nerve center so the organ falls free. Then we shall drag it to the lava before it can begin to reattach itself.
Or, we can drag it some-where else.
Johnny, cut that thing loose, please.
Sir, yes sir!
Hold on, everyone.
"I think Nepal Ho-Tep is finally feeling something we're doing!"

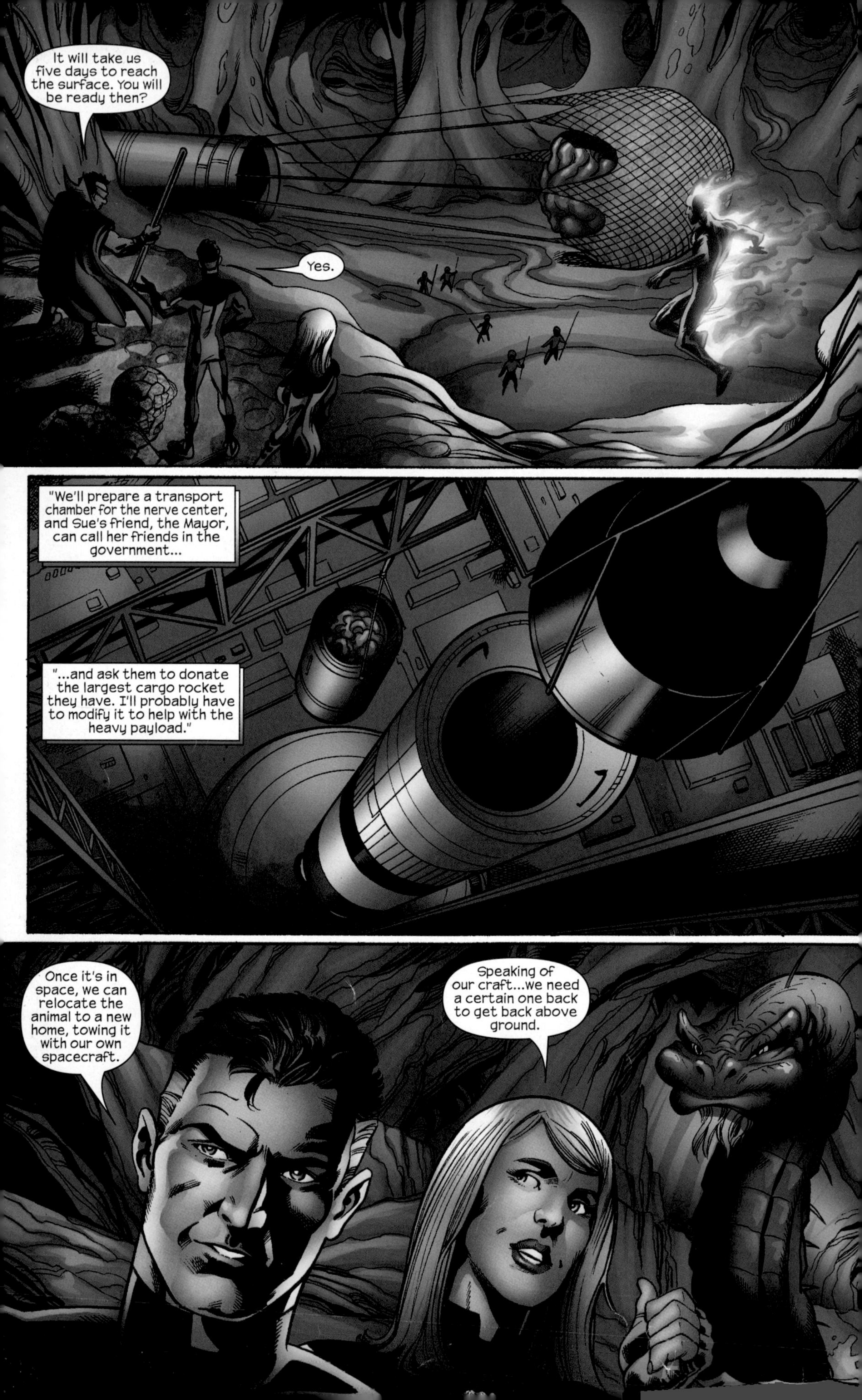
It will take us five days to reach the surface. You will be ready then?
Yes.
"We'll prepare a transport chamber for the nerve center, and Sue's friend, the Mayor, can call her friends in the government...
"...and ask them to donate the largest cargo rocket they have. I'll probably have to modify it to help with the heavy payload."
Once it's in space, we can relocate the animal to a new home, towing it with our own spacecraft.
Speaking of our craft...we need a certain one back to get back above ground.

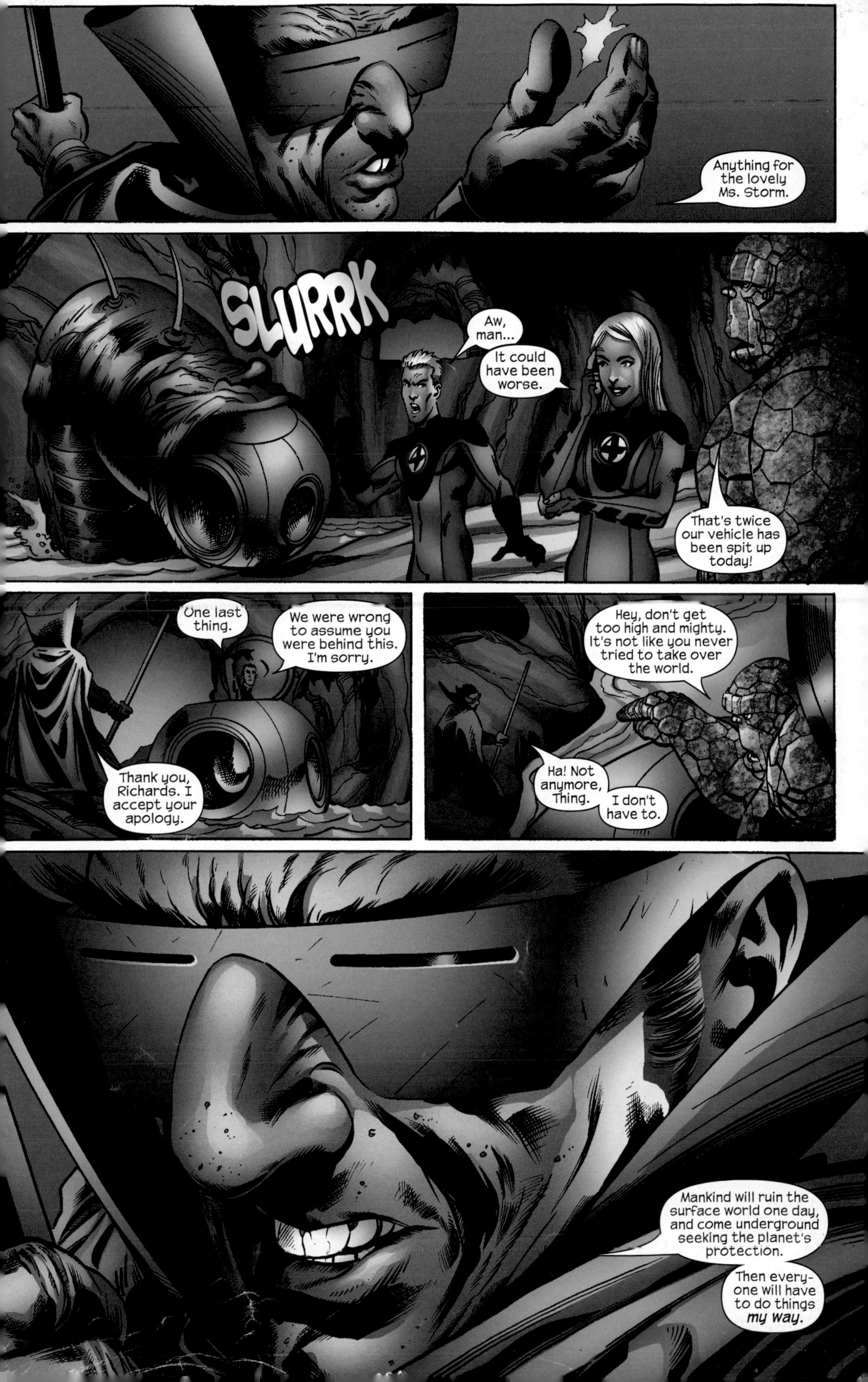
Anything for the lovely Ms. Storm.
SLURRK
Aw, man...
It could have been worse.
That's twice our vehicle has been spit up today!
One last thing.
We were wrong to assume you were behind this. I'm sorry.
Thank you, Richards. I accept your apology.
Hey, don't get too high and mighty. It's not like you never tried to take over the world.
Ha! Not anymore, Thing.
I don't have to.
Mankind will ruin the surface world one day, and come underground seeking the planet's protection.
Then every-one will have to do things *my way.*

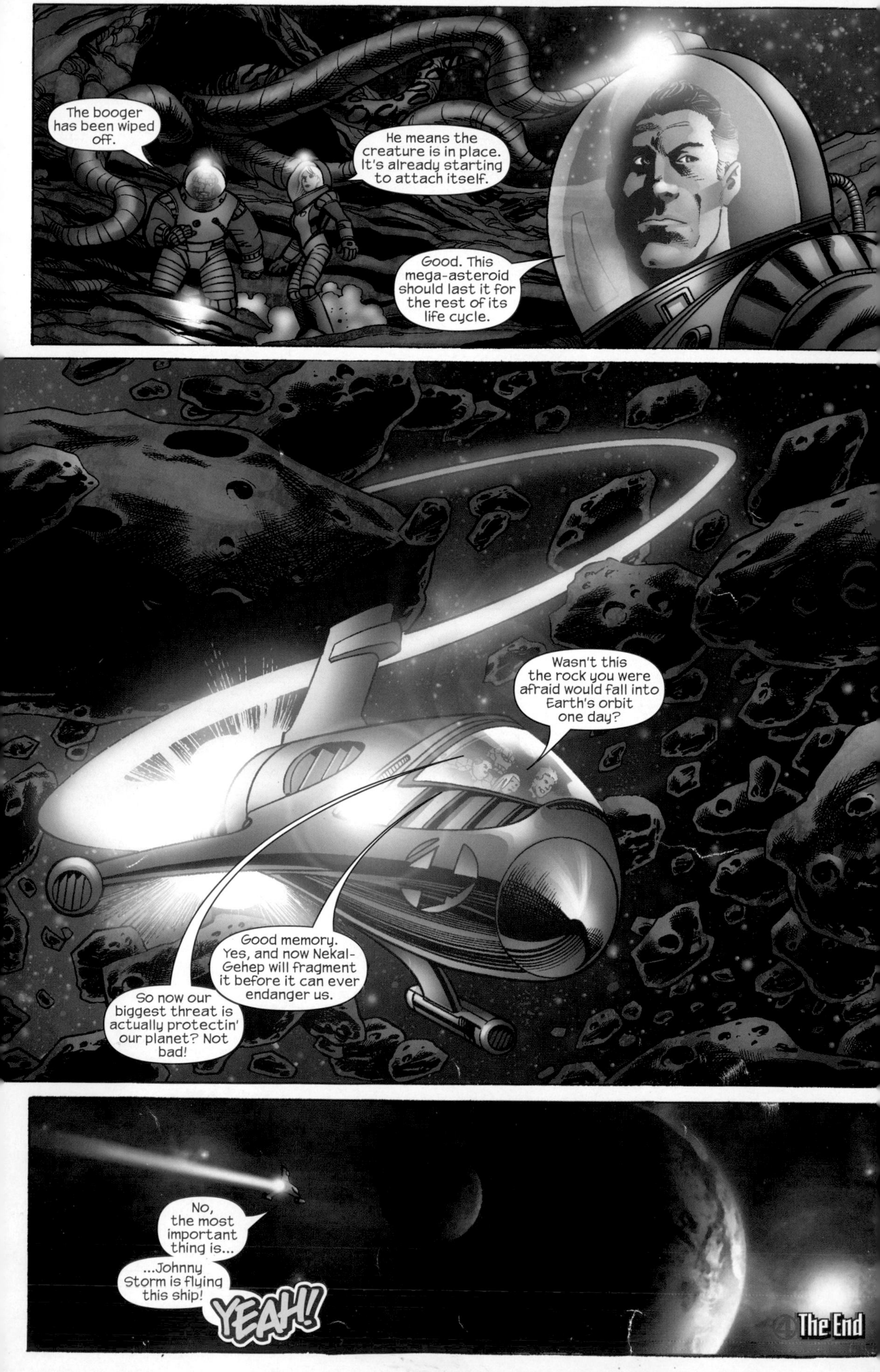
The booger has been wiped off.
He means the creature is in place. It's already starting to attach itself.
Good. This mega-asteroid should last it for the rest of its life cycle.
Wasn't this the rock you were afraid would fall into Earth's orbit one day?
Good memory. Yes, and now Nekal-Gehep will fragment it before it can ever endanger us.
So now our biggest threat is actually protectin' our planet? Not bad!
No, the most important thing is...
...Johnny Storm is flying this ship!
YEAH!!
The End